All About Me

MARVELOUS ME

Inside
and Out

Written by Lisa Bullard • Illustrated by Brandon Reibeling

Content Adviser: Lorraine O. Moore, Ph.D., Educational Psychologist
Reading Adviser: Lauren A. Liang, M.A.
Literacy Education, University of Minnesota, Minneapolis, Minnesota

PICTURE WINDOW BOOKS
Minneapolis, Minnesota

For my Alex—L.B.

Designer: Melissa Voda
Page production: Picture Window Books
The illustrations in this book were prepared digitally.

Picture Window Books
1710 Roe Crest Drive
North Mankato, MN 56003
www.capstonepub.com

Library of Congress Cataloging-in-Publication Data
Bullard, Lisa.
  Marvelous me : inside and out / written by Lisa Bullard;
  illustrated by Brandon Reibeling.
     p. cm.
  Summary: Alex is a marvelous little boy who is just like other people in
some ways, such as getting angry sometimes, but also unique because of his
special laugh, his grizzly hugs, and his own interesting thoughts.
Includes activities.
  ISBN-13: 978-1-4048-0042-7 (library binding)
  ISBN-10: 1-4048-0042-5 (library binding)
  ISBN-13: 978-1-4048-0157-8 (paperback)
  ISBN-10: 1-4048-0157-X (paperback)
  [1. Individuality. 2. Self-perception-Fiction.] I. Reibeling, Brandon, ill. II. Title.
PZ7.B91245 Mar 2003
[E]-dc21
                                                    2002008658

Printed in the United States   4316

My favorite books
and movies are about
superheroes. There's
one superhero that
I bet you don't know.
It's Marvelous Me!

ALEX

3

Marvelous Me can do super-cool things. I have legs that can race a flying football. I have eyes that can see far across the field. Doing all of these things takes a whole lot of energy. That's why superheroes have to eat their broccoli.

My brain can do super things, too.

I can read a comic book all by myself.

I can count all the cookies in the jar.

I can remember all nine planets and

the name Tyrannosaurus rex.

Marvelous me can turn the couch
into a pirate's ship and my bike
into a race car. Mom calls that
using my imagination. I call it
playing make-believe.

Playing pirate and race-car driver are only some of my favorite things. I love telling knock-knock jokes. I love polar bears and bats. I can eat more strawberry ice cream than any other superhero.

Sometimes superheroes don't feel happy. I felt sad when my best friend, Ramon, moved away. I get mad when my dog chews my toys. I feel bored when I have to clean my room. But Dad says even superheroes have to do their chores. So when I vacuum, I pretend I'm a roaring dragon.

People get confused sometimes,
because there's someone who looks
just like me. He's just my size.
He's got the same hair and eyes.
He's even got the same birthday.

He's my brother, Andy.
He's also my twin.

Andy and I may look the same to you, but our mom and dad know that we're different. Andy likes chocolate ice cream better than strawberry. I'm better at math, and he's better at reading.

Dad says we each have our own special smile.

ANDY

ALEX

Mom says it's the me inside that makes me special. Nobody else laughs like I do. Nobody else knows how to give my giant grizzly-bear hug. And only I know all the funny things inside my head.

Inside and out, I'm a super-special superhero. I'm not just Alex, I'm the one and only Marvelous Me!

There's one more superhero I think you already know. Can you guess?

It's Marvelous You!

Getting to Know You

Activity #1: Making a Marvelous Me Book

Every person is different from every other person. Your favorite things may be completely different from your best friend's. Just how well do you know yourself? How well do your family and friends know you? Try this fun activity.

1. Find three sheets of paper that are all the same size. Holding them together, fold them all in half. Staple several times along the folded edge. You have made a blank book.

2. Think about all of your favorite things. On each page of your book, draw a picture or write down one of your favorite things.

3. Here are some things to ask yourself if you need help filling all the pages:
   What is my favorite color?
   What is my favorite food?
   What is my favorite animal?
   What is my favorite game?
   What is my favorite movie?
   What is my favorite book?

4. Decorate the cover of your book and give it a title. Show your book to some people who think they know you pretty well. Were they surprised by some of your favorite things?

Activity #2: Conducting an Interview

An interview is when one person asks another person a whole bunch of questions. You might have seen a reporter interviewing somebody on television, especially on the news or after somebody wins a big game in sports. Interviews can be a good way to learn what a person is really like. Try it.

1. Get together with a friend or family member. Think of questions to ask each other during the interview and write them down. You can come up with the questions together or make your own lists.

2. Here are some possible questions:

What's your name?

How old are you?

What's your favorite color?

What's your favorite food?

Do you have any pets?

What do you like to do for fun?

3. Pretend you are doing an interview for TV, using a hairbrush or a pencil as a microphone. Take turns being the interviewer. Ask all the questions on your list, then let the other person ask you questions. Did you learn something that you didn't know before?

Words to Know

energy—power that makes something go

imagination—the ability to make things up in your mind or think of things you can't actually see

knock-knock joke—a kind of joke that always starts out, "Knock-knock!" The person who is being told the joke answers, "Who's there?" to hear the rest of the joke.

planets—large objects in space that move around the sun, such as Earth, Mars, and Venus

twins—two people or animals who grow at the same time in their mother's body and share a birthday. Some twins, like Alex and Andy, are identical, which means they also look alike.

To Learn More

At the Library

Anholt, Laurence. I Like Me, I Like You. New York: Dorling Kindersley, 2001.

Carlson, Nancy L. ABC, I Like Me! New York: Viking, 1997.

Kent, Susan. Learning How to Feel Good About Yourself. New York: Power Kids Press, 2001.

Raatma, Lucia. Self-Respect. Mankato, Minn.: Bridgestone Books, 2002.

On the Web

FactHound offers a safe, fun way to find Internet sites related to this book. All of the sites on FactHound have been researched by our staff.

Here's all you do:

Visit www.facthound.com

Type in this code: 9781404800427

Mark Lareau Tacoma, Washington.

The Nauglamir. 1½"W × 15"L.
Swarovski crystal and lampwork
bead by Matt Marchand with 20
gauge sterling silver wire.

Mark Lareau Tacoma, Washington.

Valaraukar. ¾"W × 9"L. Fluorite beads with 20 gauge gold-filled wire.

Mark Lareau Tacoma, Washington.

Cabed Naeramarth. ½"W × 21½"L plus dangle. Czech pressed glass beads and quartz crystal donut with 20 gauge copper wire.

Courtesy private collection of Helen Alvord.

Viki Lareau and Mark Lareau
Tacoma, Washington.

Belthil. 3"W × 18"L. Freshwater pearls, labradorite, and 20 gauge sterling silver wire.

Corinne Garry Bellevue, Washington.

Amethyst Dreams. ¾"W × 34"L plus dangle. Amethyst beads and sterling silver wire.

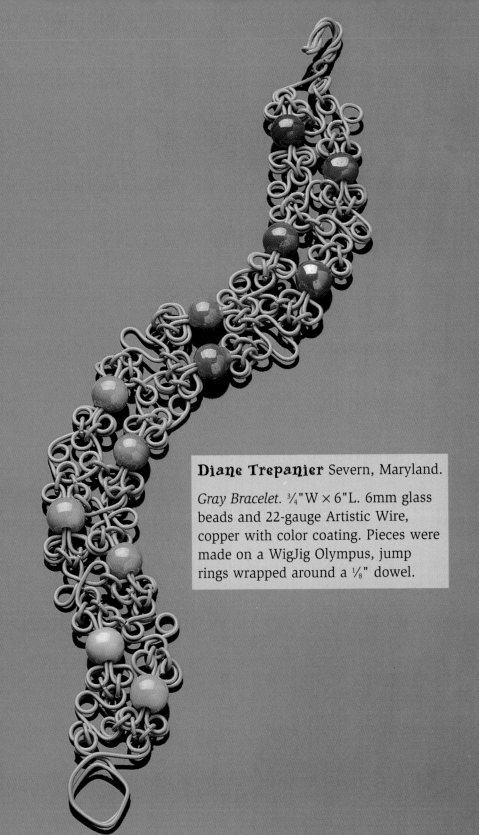

Diane Trepanier Severn, Maryland.

Gray Bracelet. ¾"W × 6"L. 6mm glass beads and 22-gauge Artistic Wire, copper with color coating. Pieces were made on a WigJig Olympus, jump rings wrapped around a ⅛" dowel.

Linda Chandler Indianapolis, Indiana.

Silver Bracelet. $^{11}/_{16}$"W × 7$^3/_4$" circumference, measured outside. Flat weave of 22 gauge pure silver wire, straight and twisted.

Kate Ferrant-Richbourg
San Mateo, California.

Silver and Stone Cuff. 1½"W × 7½" around, measured outside. Semi-precious stones and sterling silver wire.

Kate Ferrant-Richbourg
San Mateo, California.

Silver Beads and Cuff. Beads:
¾"W × 3"L and ½"W × 3"L.
Cuff: ⅝"W × 8" around, measured outside. Silver sheet,
semi-precious stones, and
silver wire.

Lynne Merchant Encinitas, California

Octopus Beads. Largest 2"W × 2"H plus chain. Sterling silver wire and beads.

Photograph by Teddy Hosman.

Lynne Merchant
Encinitas, California

Tassles. Largest
2"W × 6"H plus
chain. Sterling sil-
ver wire, beads,
and silk cord.

*Photograph by Teddy
Hosman.*

Phyllis Eagle Kalionzes
Los Angeles, California.

Tea Strainer. 2"W × 6½"L. Strainer is sterling silver wire, 24-gauge woven on 20-gauge. Handle is 14-gauge brass wire, shaped, hammered, and wrapped with 24-gauge sterling silver wire.

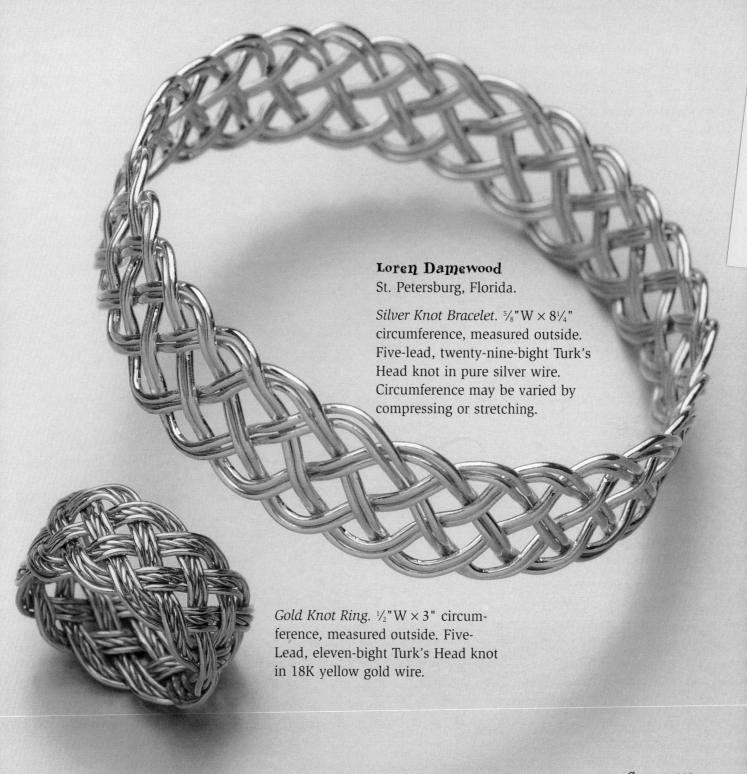

Loren Damewood
St. Petersburg, Florida.

Silver Knot Bracelet. ⅝"W × 8¼" circumference, measured outside. Five-lead, twenty-nine-bight Turk's Head knot in pure silver wire. Circumference may be varied by compressing or stretching.

Gold Knot Ring. ½"W × 3" circumference, measured outside. Five-Lead, eleven-bight Turk's Head knot in 18K yellow gold wire.

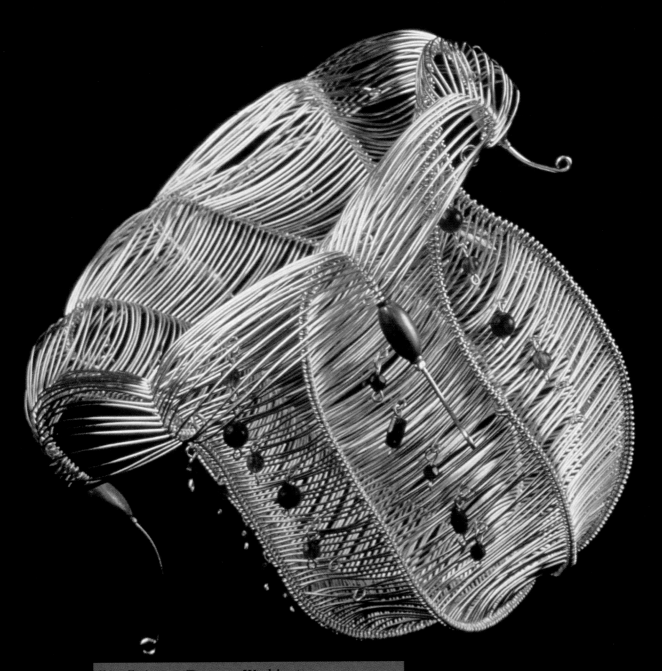

Liz Leines. Tacoma, Washington.

Spring Tulip. 5½"W × 5¾"H × 5½"D. Sterling silver wire, garnet, and amethyst.

Photograph by Ross Mulhausen.

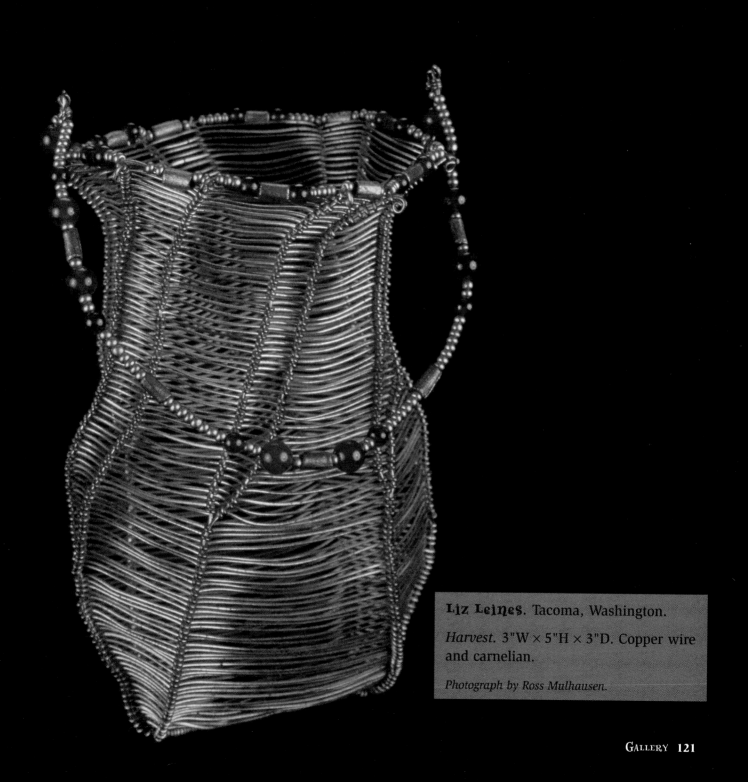

Liz Leines. Tacoma, Washington.

Harvest. 3"W × 5"H × 3"D. Copper wire and carnelian.

Photograph by Ross Mulhausen.

Kathy Moy Alhambra, California.

Choker. ⅝"W × 13"L. Green and brown freshwater pearls, new jade, and various crystals crocheted with 28-gauge soft gold-filled wire.

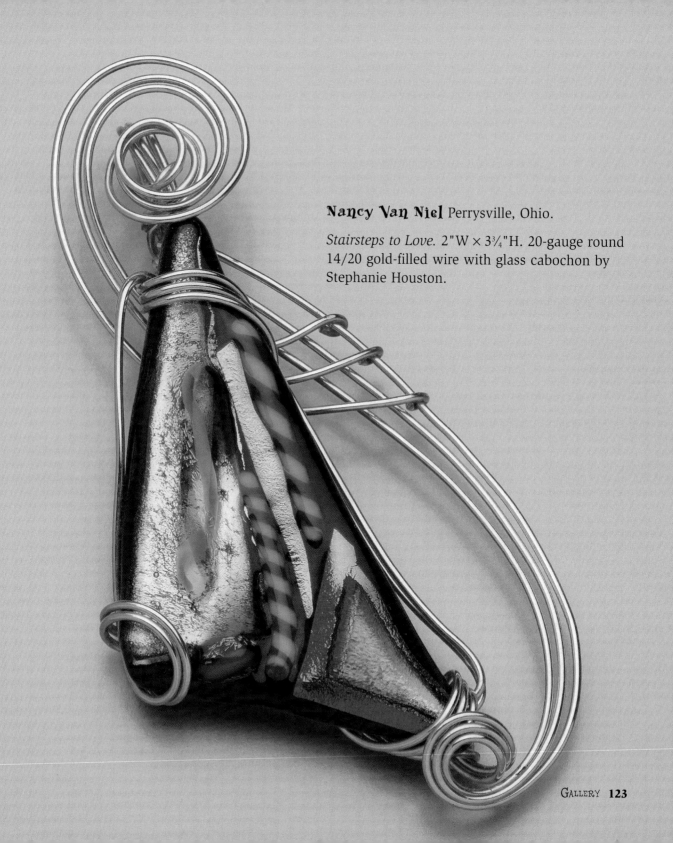

Nancy Van Niel Perrysville, Ohio.

Stairsteps to Love. 2"W × 3¾"H. 20-gauge round 14/20 gold-filled wire with glass cabochon by Stephanie Houston.

Dianne Karg Toronto, Ontario, Canada.

Triangles & Jump Rings 8-Link Bracelet.
½"W × 8"L. Sterling silver with amethyst and
hematite beads.

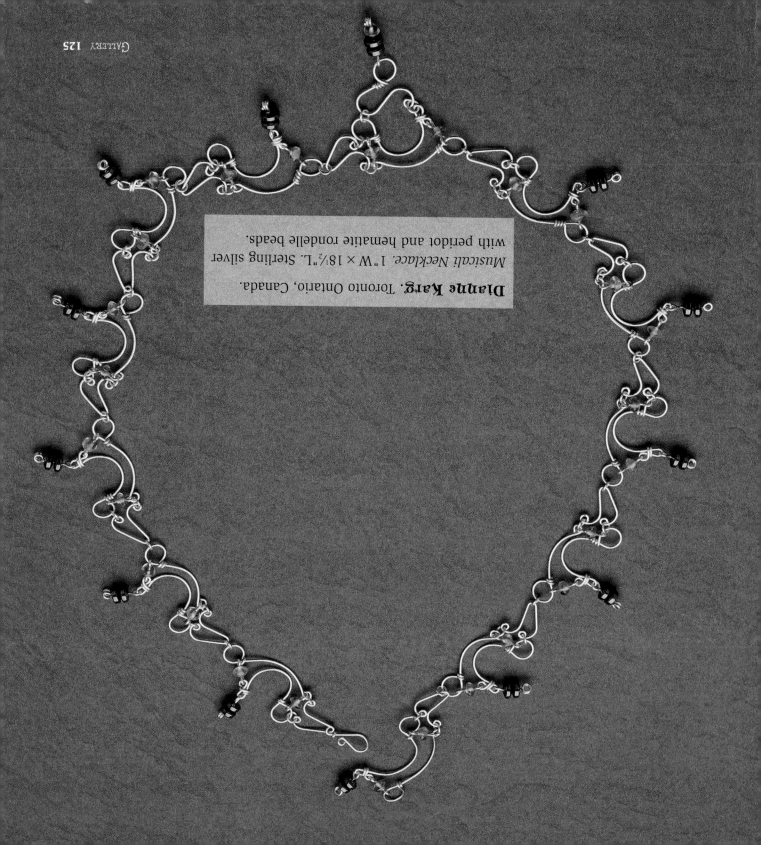

Dianne Karg. Toronto Ontario, Canada.
Musicali Necklace. 1"W × 18½"L. Sterling silver
with peridot and hematite rondelle beads.

Resources

Please support your local bead shop. Here are a few I recommend; they carry the wire, tools, beads, and supplies to help you with the projects in this book.

Baubles & Beads

1676 Shattuck Ave.
Berkeley, CA 94709
Phone (510) 644-BEAD

The Bead Factory Inc.

2601 6th Ave.
Tacoma, WA 98406
Phone (253) 572-5529
Toll Free 1-888-500-BEAD
www.thebeadfactory.com

The Bead Shop

158 University Ave.
Palo Alto, CA 94301
Phone (650) 328-7925
www.beadshop.com

Eclectica

Galleria West Shopping Center
18900 W. Bluemound Rd.
Brookfield, WI 53045
Phone (262) 641-0910
www.beads-eclectica.com

Peruvian Bead Company

461 E. Main St.
Ventura, CA 93001
Phone (805) 667-2233
www.peruvianbeadcompany.com

The Place to Bead

41 Witherspoon St.
Princeton, NJ 08542
Phone (609) 921-8050

Index

About *Beadwork*

BEADWORK magazine is devoted to every kind of bead stitching and creating. Its pages are filled with the latest innovations of the craft, including seed bead stitching, wirework, lampwork, and bead knitting, crochet, and embroidery. **BEADWORK** features beautiful photographs and drawings that illustrate projects designed by beadworkers all over the world. Its artist profiles, tips, calendar, and reviews allow readers to keep their fingers on the pulse of the international bead community.
$24 (6 issues) 800-340-7496.

Other Beadwork Books

The Beader's Companion
Judith Durant & Jean Campbell

Beader's Companion is a concise, user-friendly book that details beading techniques. It has sold over 16,000 copies.

7 × 5, spiral-bound, 104 pages. #1011—$19.95

The Best in Contemporary Beadwork
Coproduced by **BEADWORK** magazine and The Dairy Barn Cultural Arts Center

A beautifully designed art book containing work by leaders in the contemporary beadwork movement.

9 × 11, hardbound, 144 pages. #1031—$29.95

Beading on a Loom
Don Pierce

Now in its second printing, *Beading on a Loom* is a comprehensive book that covers all aspects of contemporary and historic loomweaving.

8½ × 9 paperbound, 112 pages. #1018—$21.95

Beading with Peyote Stitch
Jeannette Cook & Vicki Star

Beading with Peyote Stitch focuses on one of the most frequently used stitches in beadwork and is complete with projects and a gallery of beadwork by the authors and other nationally known artists.

8½ × 9, paperbound, 112 pages. #1027—$21.95

**Look for INTERWEAVE books at your favorite bead store,
call (800) 272-2193 or visit us online at www.interweave.com**